Kirby's Journal

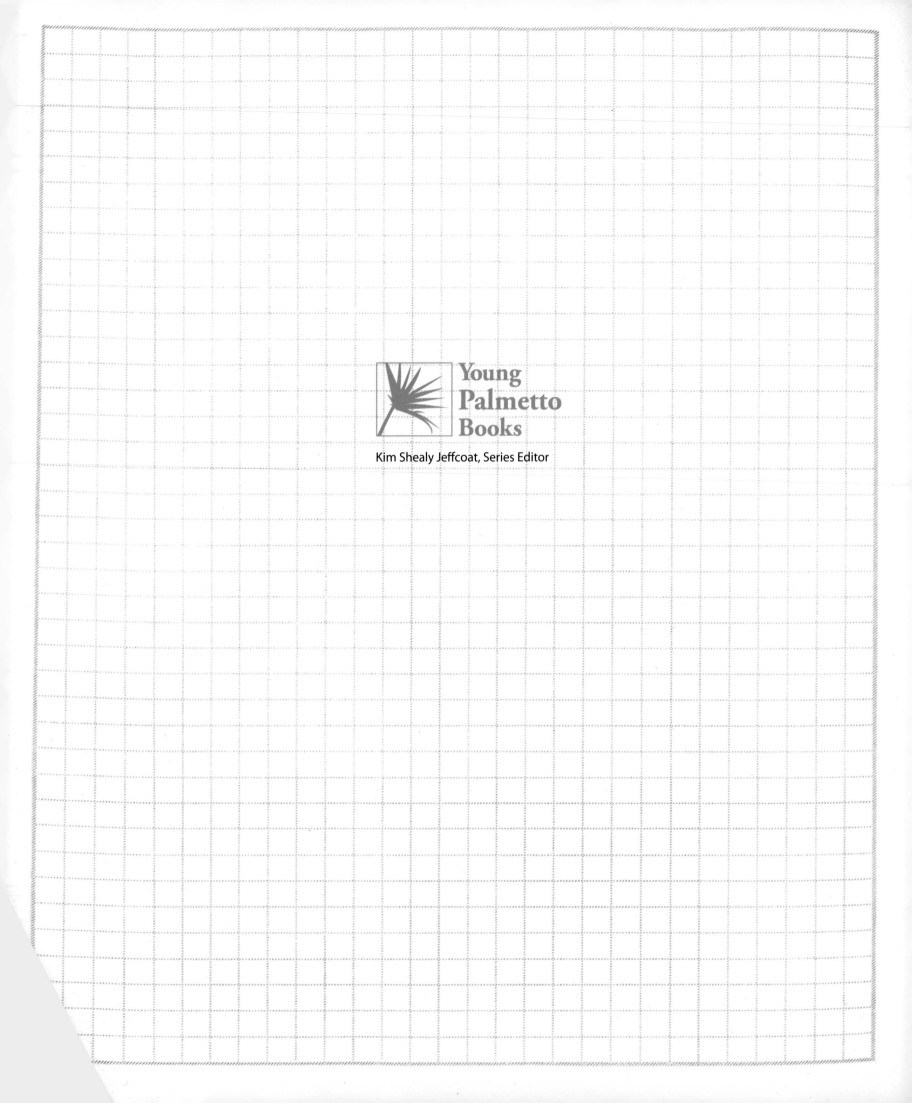

Young Palmetto Books

Kim Shealy Jeffcoat, Series Editor

Kirby's Journal

Backyard Butterfly Magic

CHARLOTTE CALDWELL

The University of South Carolina Press

© 2015 Charlotte Caldwell
Graphic designer: Gourtney Gunter Rowson, Stitch Design Co.

Published by the University of South Carolina Press
Columbia, South Carolina 29208

www.sc.edu/uscpress

Manufactured in Guangdong, China

24 23 22 21 20 19 18 17 16 15
10 9 8 7 6 5 4 3 2 1

Library of Congress Cataloging-in-Publication Data
can be found at http://catalog.loc.gov/.

ISBN: 978-1-61117-553-0 (paperback)

Photographs were taken in a myriad of locations: a Charleston, S.C., backyard and home;
Yeaman's Hall Club, S.C.; the nature trails and butterfly house of Cypress Gardens, S.C.;
Santee Delta, S.C.; Tennesee River Gardens; and the Florida Everglades.

Dedicated to my husband, Jeffrey Schutz
for his nature of nurturing and cultivating.

And to our grandchildren,
Ellie, Annie, McAlley, Hadley, and Hacker

Finally that nasty drizzle stopped. And good timing too, because today's my 11th birthday!

It was a perfect day to play outside, which was a big relief, because there was no way Mom and Dad would let us hang out inside in front of a TV or playing computer games. They're pretty old fashioned when it comes to getting " fresh air."

So my whole class came to our farm for my party. Mom tacked our black pony, Tara for rides. Dad and I dug a bunch of worms for fishing. Mom baked a pan of chocolate chip brownies—my favorite. Everyone sang "Happy Birthday" to me. I blew out all my candles and made my secret birthday wish . . . again. We had lots of fun!!

After everyone went home, Mom, Dad and I ate my favorite dinner—bacon burgers and fries. Then they gave me their presents. This journal and—just what I was wishing for—

A CAMERA

Every year they give me a journal, but this one is bigger than usual so I can tape my pictures in it too. "Journaling" is a big deal at our school. It started when we were in first grade. The first grade teacher would ask what I had done that day, and then she would write out one sentence in dots and dashes. I would trace the letters with my pencil and then draw a picture. That's first grade journaling.

Also, the teachers give us a journal-writing project over summer vacation that has to be turned in at the beginning of each new school year. I guess kids who don't go to our school think it's pretty nerdy to write in a journal. But we're used to it. I have another reason to keep a good journal this summer—my parents will be away in Africa the whole time.

They're spending the whole summer in Africa on a big job assignment. Mom's a writer and Dad's a photographer. They write books together. When I grow up, I want to be both a writer and a photographer.

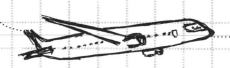

Anyway, I was hoping to go to Africa with them or maybe go to camp with my friends. But NO, I'm going to spend the whole summer with Grandma and Grampa at their home in Charleston, South Carolina.

I think it's a really bad idea, since I don't have any friends there. And nobody asked me my opinion about it. So I thought I would help them with some other ideas they hadn't thought about.

First I gave them a list of reasons Africa would be good for me.

That didn't work. So I tried this...

WHY IT'S A GOOD IDEA FOR KIRBY TO GO TO AFRICA-

- learn a lot about Africa.
- learn a lot about wild animals.
- can help carry your luggage.

WHY IT'S A GOOD IDEA FOR KIRBY TO GO TO CAMP-

- will be outside getting "fresh air"
- will get lots of outside exercise
- will be with other children- very important for healthy growth and development of social skills. (This is a big deal with all the teachers at our school.)

They didn't buy any of my ideas. Their response was:

1. too expensive   2. too expensive   3. you'll have fun with your grandparents.

Oh well, so much for my summer plans.

April 10

Today I got this from Grandma and Grampa.

Dear Kirby,

We're excited that you're coming to visit us for the summer. Moving here has been an easy transition, since your Grampa taught at the Medical University an eon ago. We really miss you and your parents though.

We hope you'll bring your tennis racket and bike because we ride everywhere. There are a bunch of kids in the neighborhood who play tennis and bike to camp down the street at the playground. You could join them if you want.

Now that he's retired, your Grampa can usually be found in his garden or bird watching. As you know, my hobby is photography. I took this picture of a butterfly when we were in the Everglades visiting your great-grandpa. This kind of butterfly is called a Queen.

Please write if you get a chance.

We love you tons,
xoxo
Grandma

P.S. We can't wait to have you here!

Grampa

Now with a letter like that, I would be a real jerk if I kept acting grumpy about spending the summer with them. They are pretty fun and don't act old and boring like some of my friends' grandparents.

So I emailed them all about how I love the picture of the butterfly and how I got a camera for my birthday, and that I hope Grandma will teach me how to take good pictures too, like she taught my Dad.

June 2nd

Yesterday I said goodbye to my friends for the summer . . . and my
pony, Tara, and the dogs and barn cats and our farm. We strapped
my bike to the car and drove to Grampa and Grandma's place in
Charleston. Their house is in the old part of the city. The houses
are real old and bunched all together. Grandma and Grampa's
backyard is TINY! It's like a secret garden surrounded by high
walls and tall holly trees, maples, and some other kind of tree with
large dark green shiny leaves.

After lunch today, Mom and Dad left for Africa. I felt really sad. Grandma gave me a big hug. Grampa
put our tennis rackets in his backpack, and we rode to the tennis courts a couple blocks away. There were
three kids who know my grandparents playing on the next court. They asked me to play with them. They
were fun!! Grandma and Grampa finished playing before we did, so I kept playing with my new pals. Then
they rode home with me. They all live right down the street. Cool.

This summer might be okay after all....

After dinner, Grandma and Grampa said they had "a little something" for me. Grandma handed me a cool
homemade WELCOME card with one of her butterfly pictures. They also gave me the new Harry Potter
book (awesome!) and a book called *Butterflies through Binoculars: A Field Guide to Butterflies of the East*
by Jeffrey Glassberg. Its called a "field guide" because when you are outside looking at a butterfly you try
to find the matching picture in the book, and then you know the name of the butterfly. I never knew there
were so many different kinds.

Then Grampa said he'd been waiting for me before starting his new project. I've never figured out what it
is about grown-ups that they always have to have a project. Grampa loves projects! He said he'd been reading
about how to create a butterfly garden and he wants me to help him. He said that it would take lots of work
to get butterflies to come to our backyard. But when they do come, Grandma said that she and I will take
lots of pictures of them and identify what kind they are with my book.

Time for bed now. It's been a very busy day. And I made three new friends, Sally, Hardy, and Francis.
(I've never heard of a boy named Francis, but I guess it's not uncommon down here. He says it is spelled
with an "is" instead of an "es".)

I woke up with the "shutter-bug itch" in my finger this morning. That's what Dad calls the "irresistible picture-taking-urge." So I took pictures of Grandma cooking breakfast, Grampa reading the paper, and our house and garden. Everything I looked at became a picture.

During breakfast Grampa explained that if we want butterflies to come to our backyard, we need to create something called a butterfly habitat.

A BUTTERFLY HABITAT

is a place that has what butterflies need

The only all-day sunny spot in our backyard is right in the middle of the lawn. Grampa said, "NO PROBLEM," so we marked off a circle and spent the day shoveling and made a round garden about two giant steps wide.

Francis came over and hung out for a while. He watched us dig and add garden soil. I gave him my shovel and told him I'd let him have a turn too. He didn't fall for that trick. He stuck around for some of Grandma's chocolate chip cookies, though, and then took off.

Grandpa's Notes— Butterfly Habitat

Food- Butterflies need particular kinds of flowers for nectar.

Water- Butterflies get water, vitamins, and minerals from moist sand or puddles.

Protection- Butterflies need protection from the wind and storms.

Our garden has high walls, so that's good.

Lots of sunshine- Butterflies need lots of sunshine to stay warm and fly.

Yikes, this might be a big problem, because our garden has mostly shade. People in Charleston might want shade in the summer, but that's not what butterflies need.

After dinner Grandma downloaded my pictures onto her computer. Most were kind of silly, but some were really funny. Grampa asked what we were laughing at. I got a funny one of him napping on the couch with his reading glasses on, a book on his chest, and his mouth wide open. Ha Ha!

Today we planted our butterfly garden.

First we went to a plant nursery, where a nice lady, Laura, helped us get the right kind of flowers for the butterflies that live around Charleston. Most butterflies sip flower nectar through their straw-like mouth, called a PROBOSCIS. But some sip juices from rotten fruit, and others will sip from dead animals or poop. YUCK!

Asclepias

Grampa's List—
Butterfly Nectar Flowers

Get colorful nectar flowers:

Zinnias, Lantanas, Pentas, Snapdragons, Asclepias (milkweed), Cosmos, Black-Eyed Susans, Cone Flowers, Bee Balm, and a butterfly bush—Buddleia.

Grampa said we don't want butterflies to "eat and run." We want them to lay their eggs in our garden, so we can watch their caterpillars grow. Caterpillars are really picky eaters! The mother butterflies will only lay their eggs on the kinds of plants their babies will eat—called HOST PLANTS. Beats me how they know which plants are the right ones.

Here's a Zebra Heliconian laying her eggs on a passion vine leaf. It's called OVIPOSITING.

Grampa's List—
Caterpillar Host Plants

HOST PLANTS—

Asclepias (milkweed) for Monarch and Queen caterpillars

Passion vine for Gulf Fritillaries and Zebra Heliconian caterpillars

Parsley, Dill, Fennel, and Moon Carrots for Black Swallowtail caterpillars

Hollyhocks for Painted Lady caterpillars

Snapdragons for Common Buckeye caterpillars

Passion vine

Grandma and I looked up all the butterflies that come to these plants in my field guide.

Laura from the nursery, said DO NOT USE  CHEMICALS in our garden, because they could kill our butterflies and caterpillars.

Well GREAT! All that work and NO BUTTERFLIES. A whole week has gone by, and we've not seen even one.

This isn't what I expected. I thought our garden habitat with its nectar and host foods would immediately bring an army of caterpillars and butterflies. (Grampa says a whole bunch of caterpillars is called an "army.") All week we've been searching for butterflies and caterpillars, especially under the leaves, because that's where they hide from danger. We've looked for caterpillar clues too, like chewed leaves. But NO. NO SUCH LUCK! Grampa says we have to be patient. But this sure is boring.

At least I have Hardy, Sally, and Francis to play with. We've had a blast. I joined tennis camp with them. Actually it's tennis, soccer, baseball and basketball camp-all down at the playground. You get to choose what you want to do. We ride our bikes down the street together every morning with our rackets and snacks stuffed into our backpacks. Hardy and I are the most evenly matched in tennis and have very long back and forth points. Our camp counselor says that Hardy and I have the same kind of tennis "strategy"—that means our plan is to let the other person make the mistake. That's why our points last forever. It's fun though.

After camp, we've all been going over to Francis's grandmother's pool to swim and cool off. Yesterday there was a bunch of old shoeboxes and other cardboard stuff piled up to be recycled. Francis got some string and scissors and four of the shoeboxes. Then we had a contest to see who could catch a squirrel. We each propped open the front of our shoebox with a stick that had a string tied to it. We baited the back part of the trap with birdseed. Then we hid and waited. Squirrels are nuts about birdseed and are pretty smart when it comes to getting into a birdfeeder for it. So we decided to tempt them with some easy goodies. And for some reason, they liked my shoebox best. Or maybe it was the way I scattered the birdseed. Or maybe I had the perfect height stick. Or maybe I kept my string straighter with no wiggles in it. Whatever it was, I perfected the squirrel-in-a-shoebox capture after only one miss. I released the poor little guy right away, and set the trap again. We caught five squirrels between us. Then they got tired of our game, or maybe they figured it out.

Another fun thing—Grandma's been showing me how to take pictures up close. It's called MACRO PHOTOGRAPHY. I didn't know how much my hands wiggled, but trying to hold the camera steady when you're getting really, really close is hard! My camera has an "anti-shake" thing-y, but Grandma showed me some more tricks like:

- put the camera on the "sports" setting, which makes it take the picture faster,
- use a flash,
- screw the camera on a three-legged stand -a tripod, so it won't jiggle.

Here's a picture I took of a bunch of newly hatched baby spiders.

On Sunday afternoon we packed our cameras, Grampa's binoculars and a picnic and hit the road to search for butterflies in their NATURAL HABITATS—like weedy areas, old fields and meadows, the outside edges of the woods, and overgrown pathways. We found lots of butterflies in those places.

Skipper

Black Racer

Duskywing

We were having so much fun
focusing on butterflies through our cameras,
that we forgot to look where we were stepping. I saw something
move near my feet, and there was a SNAKE! Here's the picture I took. When we
got home we looked in Grampa's field guide of snakes and learned it's a Black Racer.
It's not poisonous. It was probably warming itself in the sun like the butterflies were.

Cypress Gardens

Wildlife and Nature Trails

CYPRESS GARDENS $6.00 016554

CYPRESS GARDENS $6.00 016554

CYPRESS GARDENS $6.00 016555

June 14th

Sally and Hardy spent the day with us. It was a blast. We drove out to the Butterfly House at Cypress Gardens. We saw lots of butterflies flying around inside the butterfly house and outside on the nature trails. Then we saw these turtles sitting on a log in the Bald Cypress swamp.

On the way home, we stopped at a great new ice cream place. I got vanilla with crushed up peppermint stick and chocolate chips. Yum.

Yellow-bellied Sliders

Mourning Dove babies (hatchlings)

Still no butterflies or caterpillars in our garden. So I'm looking around and finding lots of other cool things to take pictures of.

Grampa's been letting me use his binoculars in the backyard to get a good look at the Mockingbirds, House Finches, and Carolina Wrens, who are all building nests and sitting on their eggs. For such a tiny yard, we sure do have lots of birds nesting. I think their favorite spot is in the hanging flower baskets on the porches. I watched a Mourning Dove sitting on her nest. She hatched these two babies.

Today, using Grampa's magnifying glass, we saw a spider do the weirdest thing. At first we thought it was dead because it was all tangled up with its eight legs pulled straight over its head. But a little while later it was fine. We got out a spider book and learned that it had MOLTED—this means it had out-grown its old skin. It had been pulling itself out of its skin, like the way I pull my sweater over my head. It was cool.

I also noticed that something was wrong with one of our plants. Its flowers were all gone.
I thought it was dying.

Then I saw them! Two Monarch caterpillars were hanging underneath some leaves! I got SO excited that I ran to get Grandma, Grampa, and my camera.
This is just what we've been waiting for

Monarch caterpillars

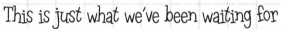

We thought caterpillars only ate the leaves. But they eat the flowers too.

MORPHOLOGY

(Body Parts)

abdomen

thorax

head

When I found the caterpillars, we couldn't figure out which end was which—the head or the rear-end. Monarch caterpillars have tentacle-like things on both ends, but they're longer and scarier looking behind their head. Grandma and I think the shorter tentacles at the rear must be a way to confuse or scare animals that might want to eat them. They sure confused me.

In school we learned about insects. So I know caterpillars are insects and all insects have three body parts—HEAD, THORAX, and ABDOMEN, and six legs. But these guys seem to have just one long body part and sixteen legs- three sets in the front and five sets behind.

Grandma and I looked in an insect book and read that the three sets on the front are the true legs, and they end in little claws. They're on the THORAX. The five other sets that look like legs are called "false legs" or PROLEGS and are attached to the ABDOMEN. Prolegs have tiny little suction-cup-hooks that keep the caterpillar from falling- good idea, since it is hanging upside-down a lot of the time.

I think I'm turning into some weirdo. It's probably so lame that I like watching caterpillars, but they're really pretty neat, especially when you watch them through a magnifying glass or close-up camera. It's funny watching them eat. Their heads swing back and forth as their jaws, called MANDIBLES, bite from side to side. They're little eating machines.

A caterpillar's head has

- a tiny set of antennae (an-ten-ee),
- a pair of chewing jaw-like mandibles,
- and six tiny eyes on each side, arranged in a semi-circle. I never could find those eyes.

When it turns into a butterfly, the body parts completely change.

A butterfly's head has

- two large compound eyes—they can see in almost every direction,
- a set of long antennae—for feeling stuff,
- and a PROBOSCIS for sipping nectar. The proboscis looks like a tiny straw when it is sipping, but it rolls up out of the way when it's not eating.

Attached to a butterfly's THORAX are

- six legs and
- four wings- two forewings and two hind wings.

It tastes and SMELLS with its feet! Grampa said my feet smell too . . . but he's kidding.

A butterfly's ABDOMEN is where the digestion, circulation, and reproduction stuff happens. And like caterpillars, they breathe through the tiny little openings on their sides called SPIRACLES.

We saw this Banded Orange butterfly at Cypress Gardens.

I measured the Monarch caterpillars yesterday, and they were 3 cm (1 ¼ in). Today they're already 5 cm (2 in.)

Grandma and I think they must have burst out of their old skins. When caterpillars outgrow their skins they MOLT—they do it about 4-6 times. Each new size is called an INSTAR.

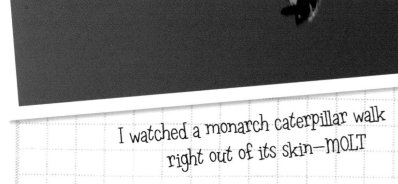

I watched a monarch caterpillar walk right out of its skin—MOLT

At camp today I told my friends about how this caterpillar walked right out of its skin. I knew they wouldn't believe me, so I showed them this picture to prove it. They biked home with me after camp to see for themselves. But this time two Monarch caterpillars put on a star performance for us. We decided they must be brother and sister, because we saw them fighting over food.

Here's what happened....

They were chomping on the same leaf, when all of a sudden the caterpillar down on the tip figured out what was going to happen. It turned around and crawled up to the other caterpillar and tried to knock it off the leaf.

The upside down caterpillar fight.

They both started waving their heads back and forth at each other, even though they were still upside-down! After about a minute, one lost and fell. The one who started the fight went back to munching. The one on the ground crawled up another plant.

My friends and I thought the whole thing was a riot.

June 23rd

My friends bike home with me after camp almost every day now. I think Grandma's homemade cookies have something to do with that. In the past three days we've found three more Monarch caterpillars on different Asclepias (ess-klep-ee-us) plants. They're all in different stages of caterpillar development.

Finally we have lots of caterpillars and butterflies action!

✸INSTARS.✸

After a week of watching our caterpillars getting fatter and fatter. . . . they're gone! I can't believe it. My friends and I searched and searched but couldn't find the fighting caterpillars. By today, all the others had disappeared, too. Grampa said they've gone to PUPATE (pew-pate). That's when they turn into a CHRYSALIS (Kris-a-liss), the last stage of development before becoming a butterfly. I sure hope our caterpillars haven't gotten eaten.

I can't believe I'm actually worrying about caterpillars.
No kidding. How weird is that!

Francis, Hardy, and I had dinner at Sally's last night. She probably has one of the coolest houses in the world, or at least in Charleston. It's a big house on a small alley near the harbor and was built during the Revolutionary War—that's a really long time ago, when the British owned America, but we fought for our independence. Her house is so old it was built before George Washington was President. It is ancient!

Sally showed us all sorts of secret hiding places and a secret corridor that took us up on top of the roof, where we looked down on the city and out across the harbor. It was so cool. Sally has three older brothers, who are all away for the summer, so she can do whatever she wants. Also, because her parents have "been through it all with her brothers," she says that as long as we don't cause too much of a ruckus, her parents don't pay too much attention to what she's doing. This is REALLY different from my house, where my parents seem to know every single thing their one-and-only is up to! They say they have eyes in the back of their heads, and I'm starting to think it's NO joke.

Anyway, playing in Sally's house is a blast, but her garden is the coolest thing- like being in a jungle. No kidding, there are so many plants hanging over into the garden paths that they hit us in the face—huge ferns, elephant ears, palm trees, lemon and orange trees, and banana trees. But coolest of all are the bubbling pools that are set into the paths. You'll fall in, if you're not watching your step. Sally's mom had the jungle garden built about five years ago and planned every single detail...except the frogs! She had all these little ponds put in to "soothe the soul," but she wasn't expecting frogs to show up to get their souls soothed too. She is scared to death of frogs! And she thinks they make such a racket that they're a nuisance. They really are so loud that you can hardly hear yourself talk.

Sally, on the other hand, loves frogs. She loves catching them. Once they started croaking, she got a sneaky, funny grin on her face and said she had a great idea. She must have caught about nine of them before we went home. It was really fun. She never told us what her idea was though. I guess she forgot about it.

July 7th

AWESOME!
Today, twelve days after the first two caterpillars disappeared, two Monarch butterflies came fluttering around from one Asclepias flower to another! I just know they're our fighting monarchs.

July 9th

Three more monarch butterflies showed up and sipped nectar from our Buddleia bush, Pentas, and Asclepias flowers.

July 11th

What a total drag. I can't believe this happened. It never occurred to me, after taking forever for our butterflies to finally show up, that they would one day just fly out of our backyard . . . and not come back. But that's exactly what they did. They just flew away! GREAT.

Monarch on Pentas

Almost ten days have passed and still NO butterflies in our backyard. NONE.

Camp is okay, but it's really HOT by 10:30 am. The death matches Hardy and I have been playing may actually cause my death if we don't get out of this heat. Thank goodness for Francis's grandmother's pool!

Grandma and I are taking pictures late every afternoon. We aren't finding butterflies in our garden, so we're watching and taking pictures of other things in our yard. I had no idea there were so many animals in such a tiny yard.

Zebra Heliconian

CLASSIFICATION
separating living things into categories based on similarities and differences

This afternoon when my friends came over, Grampa made up a "comparison game" for us to play- to see how things are alike and different in our backyard. He told us that scientists make comparisons too, and that is how they name, or CLASSIFY all living things.

Here's how we compared and classified butterflies to other living things we found in our backyard:

GRAMPA'S CLASSIFICATION NOTES

Animals and Plants are both Eukaryotes.

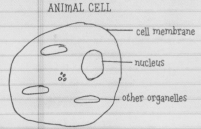

ANIMAL CELL
- cell membrane
- nucleus
- other organelles

Eukaryotes are living organisms made up of cells that have a nucleus and organelles.

Plant cells differ from animal cells because plants have a cell wall and chloroplasts.

chloroplasts
- cell wall
- cell membrane
- nucleus

PLANT CELL

First, we compared a butterfly to a flower.

Butterflies and flowers are living things, because inside each of their cells they have organelles (little compartments with special jobs) and a nucleus (the cell's brain). That's how they're alike. (Grandpa's notes help!)

But they are different because each plant cell has a cell wall and little organelles called chloroplasts. Animals don't have those chloroplast things.

Then we compared two ANIMALS in the backyard.

Like a butterfly, Grampa's dog, Phoebe, is an animal. But Phoebe is different from a butterfly because she has a backbone. She is a vertebrate.

Butterflies don't have a backbone. They are INVERTEBRATE. Instead, they have a stiff shell-like skin on the outside to give them support and protection. It's called an EXOSKELETON. When animals with an exoskeleton grow, they have to burst out of their shells. That's called MOLTING.

Grandma and Grampa's "Phoebe"

Most animals in the world are invertebrates.

Next we compared two backyard invertebrates that have jointed legs—ARTHROPODA (ar-thra-poe-duh)

Spiders, like butterflies, are invertebrates, too. They've got jointed legs, and are cold-blooded. They're grouped together because of the way their legs and feet work—ARTHRO (jointed) PODA (foot).

Golden Silk Orbweaver

But spiders are different because they have only two body segments—a head and abdomen, and eight legs—that's two more than insects. So spiders are called arachnids and butterflies are called insects.

Then we compared some INSECTS in the backyard.

Insects, like butterflies, ants, beetles, grasshoppers, and bees are similar because they all have three body parts and six legs.

Grasshopper on Asclepias

But butterflies are different from most insects because they have two sets of wings that are covered with little bitty overlapping scales, like the tiles on a roof.

Gulf fritillary wings

Bees also have two sets of wings (forewings and hind wings). But a bee's wings don't have any scales, so you can see through them.

Honey bee and snapdraggon

Next we compared two insects that have scales on their wings—LEPIDOPTERA (lep-i-dop-tera) Lepid (scaled) and Ptera (wing).

Butterflies and moths are similar because they have two sets of wings with overlapping scales.

But butterflies are different from moths because butterflies have a little club at the end of each antenna (an-ten-uh) and are awake during the daytime, DIURNAL (die-urn-ul). Moths are usually awake at night, NOCTURNAL (nock-turn-ul), and moths' antennae (an-ten-ee) are either feathery or hairy.

Also, butterflies pupate in a protective hard skin—a chrysalis.
Moths pupate in a protective silk case that they spin—a cocoon.

I've never thought about all these likes and differences before. It's cool sorting them into their separate little groups.

At that moment Grandma came outside. She had a pretty serious look on her face and told Sally that her mom had just called and that Sally was to get home—pronto. Sally grinned, and I remembered that she had something she wanted to tell us this afternoon. I guess we'll find out.

GRAMPA'S BUTTERFLY CLASSIFICATION NOTES

Domain:	Eukaryote
Kingdom:	Animalia
Phylum:	Arthropoda
Class:	Insecta
Order:	Lepidoptera

MONARCH

Family: Danaidae

Genus: Danaus

Species: plexippus

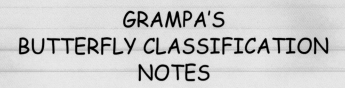

Monarch

GULF FRITILLARY

Family: Nymphalidae

Genus: Agraulis

Species: vanillae

Gulf Fritillary

If we had wanted, we could have kept going with the comparison—CLASSIFICATION—thing.
But the butterfly families and genus and species stuff got way too detailed for all of us.
And besides, Grandma just brought us some vanilla ice cream and homemade chocolate chip
cookies, fresh out of the oven. I classify her as VERTEBRATE, GRANDMA, MOST AWESOME.

So we just learned a bunch of different butterfly species by their common names, like:

Zebra Heliconian

Painted Lady

Julia Heliconian
old and tattered

Cloudless Sulfer

Black Swallowtail

Great Southern White

Queen

Red Admiral

Common Buckeye

Palamedes Swallowtail

Pearl Crescent

Francis and the gang asked Grandma to teach them how to take pictures today. That was okay with me, but then they wanted to use my camera. That's NOT so cool.

Grandma gave me THE look, and motioned with her head for me to follow her into the kitchen. She said if I'll teach my friends how to use my camera, then she'll teach me how to use her camera. Cool! I started teaching them right away!

After they FINALLY left, Grandma taught me how to take close up pictures with her camera. First she showed me how to put on the macro lens. Then we locked the camera onto the tripod. Next we opened the flash and focused by turning a ring around the lens. Focusing is the hardest part. We practiced focusing on some letters in a newspaper. Grandma manually set the camera's aperture (the opening that lets light in) and the shutter speed (how fast it opens to let light in). She said to get the sharpest close up pictures, we want the shutter speed to be as fast as it can be, because any movement blurs the focus. Then she taught me how to use a thing called a "remote shutter" so I could take the picture without touching the camera, because we didn't want the camera to move—even a hair. Grandma's camera takes a lot more thinking than mine does! But it's lots of fun.

Oh, Sally was back in camp today. We found out she got grounded from camp, telephone, computer . . . everything. She couldn't even email any of us. Ends up she was in big trouble because she took her toad frogs and placed them all over the house—inside her mother's dresser drawers, closet, kitchen cabinets. . . . you name it. Every time her mother opened a drawer, a frog would jump out. Then her mother got a "frog in her throat" (hoarse) from screaming so many times! Sally has been paying for that one. Got to admit, she just went up a couple notches in my book. Ha.

A couple days later

Hardy, Francis and Sally hung out over here thru dinner last night. Grampa picked up some farfalle pasta at the grocery store. He asked if the pasta shape reminded us of anything. He told us 'farfalla' is an Italian word that has two meanings. It means bow tie . . . and it also means butterfly.

Farfalle

So we started talking about our favorite foods and where they come from ...before the grocery store. Like:

CHOCOLATE CHIP COOKIES

chocolate—from cacao seeds—PLANT

flour—from wheat grain—PLANT

sugar—from sugar cane—PLANT

eggs—from chickens—ANIMAL

butter—from cows' milk—ANIMAL

That led to our next backyard adventure.

THE FOOD WEB—or who eats whom

Grampa said that every living thing needs energy to grow strong, to have babies, and to survive. We get our energy when we eat stuff like fruit, vegetables, bread and chicken. Fruits, veggies and bread come from plants. Plants get their energy from the sun.

PRODUCERS—Plants are called producers because they produce their energy directly from the sun. Plants produce their own energy when sunlight (PHOTO) combines (SYNTHESIZES) with carbon dioxide in the air, and water from the soil, and hits the little green things, (organelles) in the plant's cells called CHLOROPLASTS.

HERBIVORES—(HERB-plant VORES-eaters)
Animals that eat plants are called herbivores. Caterpillars eat leaves, stems and flowers of host plants. Butterflies and honeybees, sip nectar from the flowers and POLLINATE them at the same time. Animals that only get food from plants are called HERBIVORES. People who only eat plants are called vegetarians. Other herbivores in our backyard are birds that eat seeds, squirrels that eat nuts, and rabbits, that eat our neighbor's vegetables. Some herbivores NOT in our backyard are cows and elephants.

CARNIVORES—(CARN-flesh VORES-eaters)
Animals that eat other animals are carnivores. A hawk swooped down into our garden and ate a songbird. Carnivores are PREDATORS. The PREY are the ones that get eaten!

INSECTIVORES—(INSECT VORES-eaters)

Carnivores that eat insects are called insectivores. And they are really bugging me now. We found lots of them in our backyard looking for our butterflies and caterpillars!

The more we look, the more insectivores we see lurking around our backyard. Predators are everywhere! We learned about the FOOD WEB in science class, but it is totally different now that I'm in the backyard actually watching and worrying about our caterpillars.

It really bothers me that there are so many predators looking to eat our caterpillars. Grampa tried to change how I think about a prey getting eaten by a predator. This is how he explained it:

He said when an animal eats something- like when a caterpillar eats a leaf- the leaf gets RECYCLED INTO AND BECOMES the caterpillar. And when a bird eats a caterpillar, the caterpillar gets RECYCLED INTO AND BECOMES the bird. So he said we should just think of it as being "recycled," because that is what it is. He thought that would help—but it didn't! Especially since my friends and I have found a whole bunch of animals in our backyard that want to "recycle" caterpillars and butterflies, and we're not feeling too happy about it.

LIKE:

-this MOCKINGBIRD, watching a butterfly fluttering from one flower to another

-this ANOLE (lizard), an aggressive hunter

-this LYNX spider, really well camouflaged

-other insects, like this ASSASSIN BUG with its stabbing proboscis

and worst of all in our backyard were WASPS! We watched them

searching leaves and flower buds.

This wasp stung a Lady caterpillar,

chewed it into bite size chunks, and flew back to its nest with the pieces.

Another kind of wasp lays its eggs inside the caterpillar. Wasp PARASITES eat the caterpillar from inside out. YUCK!

I've gotten lots of letters from Mom and Dad. I like emailing them back and attaching some pictures.

From: kirby@kirbysjournal.com

To: momanddad@kirbysjournal.com

Cc:

Subject: July 28th – They're back!

Dear Mom and Dad,

Yesterday butterflies started coming back to our garden! I don't know where they've been, but they're back. We saw Monarchs, Gulf Fritillaries, Sulphurs, and Black Swallowtails. I'm attaching a picture I took earlier today of a Gulf Fritillary butterfly laying her eggs on passion vine stems and leaves. You can even see the little yellow egg coming out. It's called OVIPOSITING. Grampa told me that females lay hundreds of eggs, but only two or three of them survive all the way to become an adult and reproduce.

So now, when I find butterfly eggs, I bring them indoors. Grampa says it's like a greenhouse in here. I also bring in fresh host plants for the caterpillars to eat when they hatch from their eggs. But first I check that the plant doesn't have any Assassin bugs or other predators on it. Grampa says that by protecting butterfly eggs and caterpillars from predators, we are "interfering" in the natural process of the food web. But we decided that was okay.

I hope you are having fun. We are. There're lots of exciting things happening in our backyard.

I miss you.

Love, Kirby

PS. I'm glad I'm here.

Gulf Fritillary female, ovipositing

So now that our eyeballs are popping out over how many predators there are lurking and searching and desiring to "recycle" our caterpillars and butterflies, my friends and I want to know how in the world they escape getting eaten.

SURVIVAL STRATEGIES—How to avoid getting eaten!

Since plants and animals don't want to get eaten, they have to somehow ADAPT or EVOLVE (change) to protect themselves. Even plants CO-EVOLVE with the animals trying to eat them, by growing discouraging stuff like thorns or lots of hairs, or producing chemicals that are poisonous.

Caterpillars have EVOLVED ways to protect themselves. These Black Swallowtail caterpillars are wet and gooey looking during their early instars when they are small. The colors are arranged on them in a way (COLOR PATTERNS) to make them look like bird poop! Not too tasty! Hopefully, it works.

Black Swallowtail caterpillars—early instars

Black Swallowtail caterpillar displaying osmeterium

Some caterpillars have nasty, stinky tentacles that pop out from behind their heads and spray yucky smelling stuff at their attackers. It's called an OSMETERIUM. This Black Swallowtail caterpillar sprayed me, and it really stinks!

Gulf Fritillary caterpillars have prickly barbed spines to keep predators away from them

Lots of butterflies have evolved color patterns to CAMOUFLAGE or hide themselves. This butterfly is called a Question Mark. It's camouflaged to look like a dead leaf.

My arrow is pointing to the tiny "?" on the wing of the Question Mark butterfly.

Some caterpillars and butterflies have toxins (poisons) in their blood. Certain colors, like yellow, black, orange, and red warn predators that they're poisonous— WARNING COLORS.

These Monarch caterpillars have yellow, white, and black bands of warning.

A Monarch butterfly has orange and black warning colors. Any bird that tries to eat a Monarch will puke!! No kidding.

Viceroy

This is a Viceroy. It avoids getting eaten by being a copycat of (MIMICING) the warning colors of the Monarch. Some caterpillars use mimicry too, like the Spicebush Swallowtail which mimics the head of a snake. Birds don't want to mess with a snake because snakes will "recycle" birds into snake.

These Common Buckeyes have color patterns on their wings that look like big eyes, but they are fake. They are called FALSE EYES and protect butterflies and caterpillars in a couple ways. First, large eyes might scare a predator.

Common Buckeye

Also, birds usually bite at the meaty head where the eyes are. But the false eyes are a trick, so the bird will only get a bite of scaly wing. We saw this White Peacock butterfly with a perfect beak-bite taken out of its wing.

bird beak-bite on the White Peacock

hiding White Peacock

Caterpillars and butterflies also have other ways to protect themselves. This White Peacock is protecting itself by hiding on the underside of a leaf.

Also, butterflies do most of their flying around in the middle of the day when the sun is shining and warm. That helps them avoid birds, because birds usually eat early in the morning and again later in the afternoon.

Also, butterflies have really good eyesight and can see almost all the way around them. So they have a chance to see and escape a predator.

August 14

We had the best time last night. A bunch of us hung out over at Hardy's house for a barbeque. Hardy's dad brags about his pulled pork, barbeque ribs, collard greens, and barbeque sauce concoctions. I think it's a really Charleston kind of meal. Anyway, it was his birthday, so he threw himself a big neighborhood party. It was lots of fun.

After dark the lightning bugs came out and were flashing their tail lights all over the backyard. Then the jars came out too, with holes poked in the lids, so the lightning bugs could breathe. Then the competition began to see who could collect the most lightning bugs. There were about eight of us kids running all over the place trying to catch lightning bugs. When it was time to go home, we counted up our catches to see who won. Wouldn't you know it, Sally won by a long shot. She collected twenty-three of them. Everyone started releasing them before going home. Except Sally. She asked me and Francis and Hardy if she could have ours too. That gave her about fifty of them, total, because a few of them escaped during the transfer to her jar.

As she stuffed the jar into her backpack, she had that up-to-no-good-smile on her face again. This time I asked what's up. She said it gets very dark and lonely in her room at night, so she was going to release them in her bedroom before her mom came to kiss her goodnight. Then she gave me a big smile, and turned to walk home with her parents.

Sally didn't get grounded this time and that's good, because there is so much butterfly stuff going on, that no one wants to miss any of it. My friends come home with me right after camp every day now.

SPECIAL SURVIVAL BEHAVIORS

Grampa told us that predators aren't the only problem butterflies have. They're cold-blooded, which means their body temperature is the same as the outdoor temperature, and that's a real problem if it's cold. The problem is that butterflies can't fly until the blood-like stuff (HEMOLYMPH) in their wing muscles warms up to between 75-110 degrees Fahrenheit. So when the temperature is below 75, they must BASK and SHIVER to get warm.

This Zebra Heliconian is BASKING in the sun with its wings extended. Its wing scales are dark, so it's able to absorb more heat from the sun.

Sometimes butterflies will shake their wings really, really fast. It looks like, so it's called SHIVERING, but they're actually doing butterfly jumping jacks to warm up their muscles.

basking Zebra Heliconian

A flower's nectar has lots of sugar for energy.

nectaring Spicebush Swallowtail

But it doesn't have some important vitamins and minerals that butterflies need. Boy butterflies will sip minerals and salts from moist puddles and sand. Today we saw this male Palamedes Swallowtail PUDDLING.

puddling Palamedes Swallowtail

Males pass those vitamins and minerals along to females when they mate. These are mating Monarchs. Although they are pretty well camouflaged, they can fly while they are mating, if they have to escape a predator.

mating Monarchs

Butterflies look for a mate by going to the top of a hill to get the best view. It's called HILLTOPPING. Another way they'll find a mate is by PATROLLING back and forth on paths, like these Common Buckeyes. After they mate, the female starts looking for a host plant where she can lay her eggs.

patrolling Common Buckeye

SURVIVAL—Weather and Seasons

In really bad weather, butterflies and caterpillars try to survive by finding shelter and hiding. Grampa says that in the cold climates, most butterfly species spend the winter (OVER-WINTER) by entering a stage of insect hibernation called DIAPAUSE. It's like taking a "time-out" or pausing from development. They can do it when it's really hot and dry too.

Some butterflies, like Monarchs, Red Admirals, and Painted Ladies, survive the winter weather by MIGRATING to a warmer climate. Last year my class read a book about the fall brood of Monarch butterflies and how they migrate to a special habitat in the mountains of central Mexico for the winter. Tens of millions of them spend the winter there in large roosts on a certain type of fir tree called the Oyamel Fir. The next spring, those same adults, who by then have lived six months or more, start their journey back to their summer homes. On the way home, they mate, lay their eggs, and die. The next GENERATION, their kids, continue the journey. Then they mate too, lay their eggs, and die. Then the next generation keeps going.

It's amazing to think that next spring some of the children or grandchildren of the Monarchs that migrated from our backyard last fall might come back to this very same area—maybe even our yard! It's so mysterious. How do they know their way?

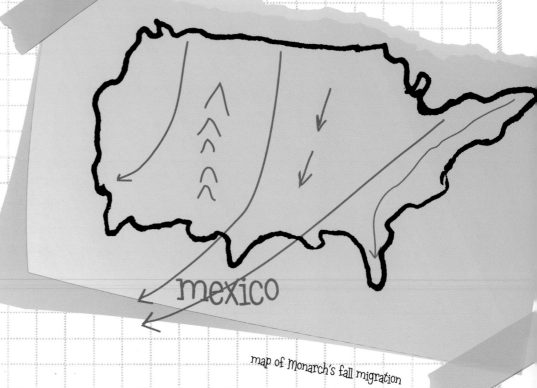

map of Monarch's fall migration

Assassin bug and molted skins

For the last three weeks Grandma and I've been taking pictures of the LIFE CYCLE OF BUTTERFLIES— COMPLETE METAMORPHOSIS. I learned this stuff in school, but it's totally different when you get to watch it happening naturally.

All insects develop from an egg to an adult by changing shape. META (change) MORPH (shape). Grampa explained to my friends and me that some insects, like grasshoppers, cockroaches, and this Assassin bug develop from an egg to an adult by simply molting - bursting out of their old exoskeleton. They might do this a half dozen times before they reach adulthood. Their change is called INCOMPLETE METAMORPHOSIS.

Other insects, like butterflies, dragonflies, bees, flies, and beetles go through a COMPLETE and total change, not only in how they look, but also where they live and what and how they eat. They are so different in their stages of development that we even call them by different names.

BUTTERFLY LARVAE (lar vee) are called caterpillars.

A BUTTERFLY PUPA (pew-pa) is called a chrysalis

CHRYSALIS (kris-a-liss) comes from a Greek word that means gold. If you look closely, there's a little gold speck spun into the chrysalis.

The pupa of a moth is called a COCOON.
There's no gold spun in a cocoon

COMPLETE METAMORPHOSIS

Between being a caterpillar (the larval stage) and a butterfly (the adult stage) it has a pupal stage.
When it pupates inside its chrysalis, it undergoes something called
COMPLETE METAMORPHOSIS

Grampa explained that COMPLETE METAMORPHOSIS is a circle that keeps going from egg to larva to pupa to adult. Each complete cycle is called a GENERATION or BROOD. Depending on the climate and the type of butterfly, there may be four or five broods every warm season—like a Monarch in Charleston, or only one brood every fourteen years—like the Arctic Woolly Bear.

FIRST a female lays her eggs on the right kind of host plant. Here's a Gulf Fritillary egg that has been laid on the tendril of a passion vine host plant. With macro photography, I magnified it more than ten times. It's actually really tiny, like the period at the end of this sentence.

NEXT the caterpillar (larva) pops out of the egg.
I watched this little bitty Gulf Fritillary caterpillar emerge from its egg.
It must have really been squished inside, because when it came out it was three times the size of the egg.

Its little spines stuck up in less than five minutes. Then it ate its egg!

FINALLY an adult butterfly comes out, emerges from the chrysalis and flies with four wings and sips food through its straw-like PROBOSCIS. It has COMPLETELY changed its shape, the way it moves and eats. A very different critter from when it was a caterpillar.

Now I understand why its called COMPLETE METAMORPHOSIS.

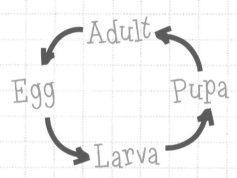

Adult

Egg   Pupa

Larva

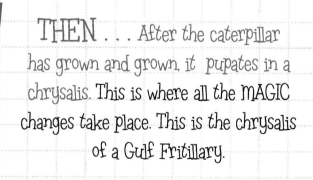

THEN . . . After the caterpillar has grown and grown, it pupates in a chrysalis. This is where all the MAGIC changes take place. This is the chrysalis of a Gulf Fritillary.

All summer my friends and I have been getting up close and watching the tiniest things in our backyard. It's so fun, because it's like having an adventure and experiencing something really cool. And all we do for this exploration is walk out the back door and look. LOOK AND WATCH.

Here's an egg that a Monarch female laid on an Asclepius flower.

Some butterflies lay eggs in clusters. The eggs in the center of the cluster are most protected from predators and weather.

Out of the hundreds of eggs a female lays, only a couple of them survive all the way to adulthood!

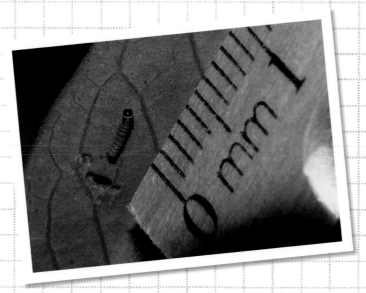

This Monarch caterpillar has just hatched from its egg. Now Grandma and I understand why we had so much trouble finding our first Monarch caterpillars.

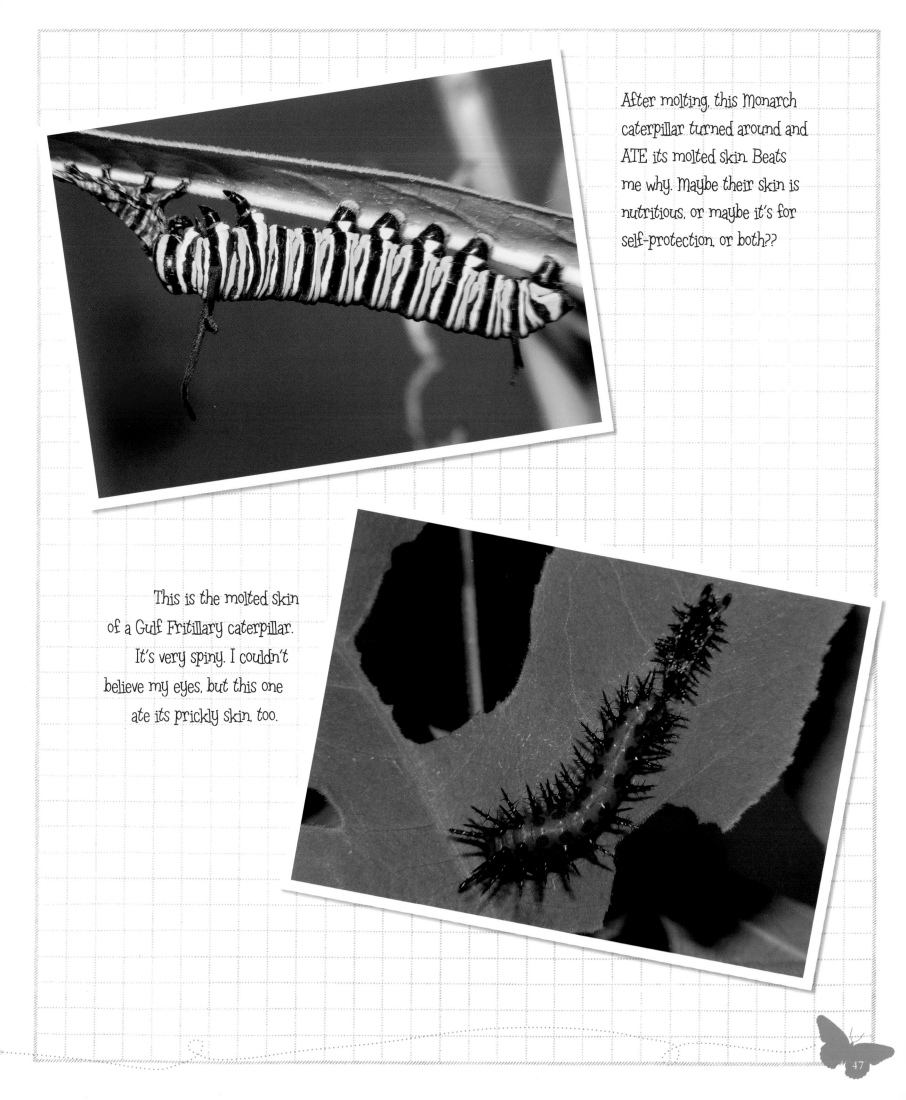

After molting, this Monarch caterpillar turned around and ATE its molted skin. Beats me why. Maybe their skin is nutritious, or maybe it's for self-protection, or both??

This is the molted skin of a Gulf Fritillary caterpillar. It's very spiny. I couldn't believe my eyes, but this one ate its prickly skin, too.

When the caterpillars became full-grown, we watched them search and search for a perfect spot to pupate. Black Swallowtails pupate in an upright position.

This Black Swallowtail caterpillar has just begun the process of becoming a chrysalis. I can see the silk it has spun to hold it in position.

This is the same Black Swallowtail less than twenty-four hours later. As its chrysalis hardened, it became more and more camouflaged to look like the stick.

Most caterpillars hang upside-down and curl into a "J" position to pupate, like this Gulf Fritillary.

Within an hour it started to vibrate and swing in a circular motion, wriggling out of its last caterpillar skin. Its last spiny skin is wrinkled at the top, about to be shoved away by its swinging motion.

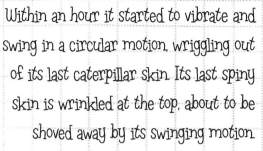

Then some kind of coating started to ooze out of its skin.

By the next morning, that coating had changed colors, hardened to form a chrysalis and now it was completely camouflaged to look like the dead leaves and sticks around it.

Because butterflies are completely defenseless in their pupal stage, camouflage is their best defense for survival.

Today I skipped camp. I even skipped my normal big breakfast. I also skipped brushing my teeth (but that's not too unusual.) Grampa laughed at Grandma and me and said we were on a "Monarch Vigil." Grandma whispered that yes, we were, and also we're "cultivating patience." Because there's NO WAY we would think of missing a second of what's about to happen here. A Monarch is going to emerge from its chrysalis.

I don't have a clue how it happens, but somehow major changes take place inside the chrysalis. The caterpillar's body chemicals—HORMONES—change what had been a caterpillar into a butterfly. mAGIC!!!

We knew it was about to happen, because about a day before a Monarch butterfly emerges, its chrysalis changes colors. The bright green becomes very dark and see-through. We could make out the wings, proboscis and antennae through the chrysalis casing.

10:25:38 AM
Cracking the chrysalis open

10:27:12
swinging free

First it cracked the chrysalis open. It kept pushing in opposite directions with its head and legs.

Monarch chrysalis with specks of gold and last molt on top.

10:26:07 Legs Pushing

It's amazing, that less than two weeks ago I had watched a huge three-inch caterpillar encase itself into a one-inch chrysalis, and today it emerged.

Then it swung free. I thought it was going to fall, but it grabbed the empty chrysalis with its feet.

10:32:47
Fluid from abdomen pumps into wings veins

10:43:47 wings expanding.
Front and back wings visible

Slowly its abdomen started getting smaller as its wings got larger. It pumped its blood-like fluid —HEMOLYMPH—from its abdomen into its wing veins.

10:28:17 huge abdomen, tiny wings

At first it was a strange looking creature with tiny wings and a HUGE abdomen.

IN LESS THAN EIGHTEEN MINUTES after it cracked open its chrysalis . . . it BECAME a large beautiful Monarch butterfly.

A butterfly's in big danger from its predators when it first emerges from the chrysalis. It can't fly for at least an hour, maybe longer, depending on how warm and sunny it is. We watched our Monarch's first flight. It was very rickety and wobbly. We were glad no hungry predators were around.

Grandma and I agree that
taking time to watch nature is really worth it!

WOW!!!!!

HABITAT CONSERVATION

By building our backyard butterfly habitat and by not using chemical pesticides, we helped BUTTERFLY CONSERVATION.

Over the summer, we watched and learned how hungry predators and harsh weather are big problems for butterflies and caterpillars. But people can also be a major hazard to their survival! BUTTERFLY HABITATS—fields, meadows and woodlands—are being destroyed for lots of buildings. It's important that we protect some land for butterflies and other insects and wildlife.

Butterflies and other invertebrates are very important to the whole food web. We need them too, because they pollinate a lot of the plants that we eat. They are also beautiful and lots of fun to watch.

Pesticides and pollution are really bad for them. They can make some types of butterflies die and disappear forever—go EXTINCT. We're glad that we had been warned that chemicals could harm our butterflies and caterpillars.

Mom and Dad are back from Africa. They came right to Charleston.

I'M SO EXCITED !!

This morning at breakfast they asked me what was my favorite thing about the summer.

FIRST PLACE:

Hardy, Francis, and Sally

NEXT PLACE . . . I decided to show them. I led them down the path to the backyard and asked what they saw. There was our tiny round butterfly garden in the center of the yard.

I took them a little closer and asked
them to look very carefully.

There was a single passion
vine leaf with a dot on it.

Then I gave them a magnifying glass,
so they could get a really close look.

The little dot was an egg.
A Gulf Fritillary egg with a

WHOLE LIFE INSIDE IT!

I told them that my new friends and I went on safari every day, right in our own backyard. All we had to
do was look, watch, explore, and get excited about all the stuff happening in our garden. There's a whole
zoo-full of life happening right here in one tiny space. An adventure.

And of course, I really liked spending time with Grandma and Grampa, and learning
to take pictures of what I saw.

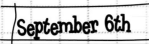
I'm back home now. School starts in a couple days. Nothing about my summer turned out like I expected. I miss my new Charleston friends, Grandma and Grampa and exploring in their tiny backyard.

I got this postcard from Grandma and Grampa today.

Sept. 4th

Dear Kirby, –
Our naturalist, conservationist, and photojournalist,

We loved sharing the backyard butterfly magic with you. We hope next summer we can explore other adventures together.

Isn't it amazing that such awe-inspiring surprises, metamorphosis, and wonders occur in life, right in our own little backyard!
We miss you and love you tons,
    Xoxo
    Grandma and **Grampa**

PS. Your friends stop by to check on the butterfly garden almost every day. They miss you, and our chocolate chip cookies, too.

PPS Keep a lookout for the tin of goodies in the mail to you.

Common Buckeye
USA 24
2006

Kirby
Rising Fawn Farm
Earlysville, Virginia
22936

I emailed them back immediately.

From: kirby@kirbysjournal.com

To: grandma@kirbysjournal.com

Cc:

Subject: Sept. 7 – Thanks

Dear Grandma and Grampa,

Thank you for the most fun summer a kid could ever have!
I hope I can come again next summer.

I miss you, and my new friends.

I also miss our backyard safaris. We discovered a whole world of adventure there!

Love,
Kirby

PS Dad served us the butterfly pasta for dinner tonight.

PPS Momma said my feet smelled. I started laughing and said butterflies' feet smell too.
She looked at me like I was crazy. Ha ha.

I love you,
Kirby

ACKNOWLEDGEMENTS

There are so many people who have taken the time to read, provide encouragement,
insights, direction, and constructive criticisms for *Kirby's Journal.* Among those I'd like to thank are:

Authors: Bill McKibben, Richard Louv, Linda Lear, Wes Jackson, Tim Cahill, Dorothea Benton Frank and
Susan Ewing. Poets : Marjory Wentworth, Poet Laureate of S.C., and Barbara Hagerty.

Naturalists, entomologists, biologists: Dr. Bruce Coull, dean of University of South Carolina's School for the
Environment; Dr. Mitchell Thomashow, former chair of the Doctoral Program in Environmental Studies at Antioch
University New England; Dwight Williams, director, Cypress Gardens, Moncks Corner, S.C.; Rudy Mancke, whose
South Carolina nature field trips are always an enlightening adventure; and Lisa Lord, wildlife biologist
for Beaufort County Open Land Trust.

Garden expert: Laura George at Hyams Garden Center, Charleston, S.C.

Librarians, teachers, students: Mimi Seyfert, librarian, and Virginia Reed, fifth grade teacher and director of Lower
School and students of Charleston Collegiate School, Johns Island, S.C.; Mary Bryan Granzow, librarian and her
students at Wood Gormley Elementary School, Santa Fe, N.M.; Cindy Thomashow, director of
environmental education program at Antioch, N.E.

Friends: Laura Gates; Pete Wyrick; Virginia and Dana Beach; Penelope Pierce; Whitney Tilt; Bob Caldwell;
Julia Moe; Jane Preyer, North Carolina regional director of Environmental Defense Fund; Bob Perkowitz,
chairman ecoAmerica; and Richard Louv, author of *Last Child In the Woods.*

Special thanks goes to:

Anne Cleveland, director of the South Carolina Library Society, for generously and tirelessly helping me revise, revise,
and revise the text; Antioch University New England where I received my masters in environmental studies, and learned
to love entomology; Betsy Bishop for fresh eyes, ideas, and spirit; and graphic designer Courtney Gunter Rowson, for
her creativity, patience, and grasp of Kirby's character.

My son, Hacker Burr, head of school at Charleston Collegiate School
and his wife, Steph, a mother and forever teacher.

My son, Bunker Burr for "babysitting my caterpillars" on more than one occasion.

My mom, Harriet Caldwell, who cultivated beautiful gardens and many children, and never let us play indoors.

My father, Hardwick Caldwell, who instilled in me, at an early age,
the love of observing and exploring the outside world.

My husband, Jeffrey, for building our butterfly garden and supporting my project. I am especially grateful for his
nurturing, enriching, and cultivating soils and souls with encouragement to turn dreams into realities.

Arnett, Ross H., Jr., Jacques, Richard L. Jr. *Simon & Schuster's Guide to Insects*. New York: Simon & Schuster, 1981.

Burris, Judy, Richards, Wayne. *The Life Cycles of Butterflies*. North Adams, Mass: Storey Publishing, 2006.

Cech, Richard and Tudor, Guy. *Butterflies of the East Coast*. Princeton: Princeton University Press, 2005.

Imes, Rick. *The Practical Entomologist*. New York: Simon & Schuster, 1992.

Kaufman, Kenn, and Brock, Jim P. *Butterflies of North America*, Boston: Houghton Mifflin Company.

Golden Guide. *Spiders and Their Kin*. New York: St. Martin's Press, 2002.

Glassberg, Jeffrey. *Butterflies through Binoculars, A Field Guide to Butterflies of the East*. New York: Oxford University Press, 1999.

Pringle, Laurence. *An Extraordinary Life-The Story of a Monarch Butterfly*. New York: Orchard Books, 1997.

Stokes, Donald and Lillian. *Stokes Field Guide to Birds, Eastern Region*. Boston: Little, Brown and Company, 1996.

North American Butterfly Association's quarterly magazine, *Butterfly Gardener*.

Wagner, David L. *Caterpillars of Eastern North America*. Princeton: Princeton University Press, 2005.

Xerces Society/Smithsonian Institution. *Butterfly Gardening*. San Francisco: Sierra Club Books, 1990.

AN INDEX

of some of the words in my journal.